Drabble Harvest: Space Station Duty Free

Edited by Terrie Leigh Relf

DRABBLE HARVEST IS EDITED BY TERRIE LEIGH RELF

All rights reserved. No part of this book may be reproduced or transmitted in any form or by any means, electronic or mechanical, including photo-copying or recording or by any information storage and retrieval systems, without expressed written consent of the author and/or artists. Any similarity between places and persons mentioned in the fiction or semi-fiction and real places or persons living or dead is coincidental.

Story copyrights owned by the respective authors

Cover Art "Big Rig" and cover design by Laura Givens

Drabble Harvest is published twice a year, in conjunction with The Hiraeth Publishing Drabble Contests

Contents

5 A Little Help, Please
10 Editorial by Terrie Leigh Relf
11 Somehow We've Got to Force the Legislature to Clamp Down on These Human Trafficking Companies by Francis W. Alexander
12 A Hair-Brained Scheme by Christine Witten
13 Spacestation Romeo by Tom Duke
16 Entry Denied by Joseph Sidari
17 The Perfect Duty-Free Gift by Margarida Brei
21 Alpha Centauri Space Station Duty-Free: Incident Register by Charlotte Kowalski
22 Coyote by Jeff Currier
23 A Million Holes: Einstein Would Be Proud by Gary Davis
26 Synapsers by Denise Hatfield
27 The Rough Side of Space by Marcia A. Borell
28 Gizm-oh-no-you-DON'T! by Kristin Lennox Mill
29 Caveat Emptor by Greg Schwartz
31 Contraband by Scott O'Neill
32 Nothing to Declare by Greg Beatty
33 Duty-Free Import? by D. L. R. Frase
34 Two Customs Agents Settle a Regulatory Dispute by Roger Johns
36 If I Could Save Time in A Bottle by Iseult Murphy
37 Down to Earth by N. E. Rule
39 The Trafficking of TEs by Reen Trusteven's Subordinate by sakyu

SALE AT HIRAETH PUBLISHING!!!

THERE'S A SALE GOING ON!!!
IT'S STILL GOING ON!!!

BUY ALL THE BOOKS YOU WANT AND USE THIS 20% DISCOUNT CODE:

BOOKS2023

(after 1 Jan 24, the code is BOOKS2024)

GO TO OUR SHOP AT
WWW.HIRAETHSFFH.COM

NO MASKS, NO WAITING, AND WE NEVER CLOSE!

From the desk of the deputy assistant adjutant to the Boortean Ambassador

A Little Help, Please

In the world of the small indie press we fight a never-ending battle for attention to our work, as writers and in publishing. Here's an example: big publishers [you know who they are] have gobs of $$$ that they can devote to advertising and marketing. Here at Hiraeth Publishing, our advertising budget consists of the deposits for whatever soda bottles and aluminum cans we can find alongside the highways. Anti-littering laws make our task even more difficult . . . ☺

That's where YOU come in. YOU are our best promoter. YOU are the one who can tell others about us. Just send 'em to our website, tell them about our store. That's all. Just that.

Of course, we don't mind if you talk us up. We're pretty good, you know. We have some award-winning and award-nominated writers and artists, plus other voices well-deserving to be heard [not everyone wins awards, right?] but our publications are read-worthy nevertheless.

That number once again is:
www.hiraethsffh.com

Friend us on Facebook at Hiraeth Publish

Follow us on Twitter at @HiraethPublish1

Iuliae: Past Tense
By Tyree Campbell

Two sisters of the Iulius Family have run away from the restrictions and rules of their settlement on a remote world, and embark on a journey of discovery, to learn what to do with their new-found freedom. Along the way, they become smugglers, and opponents of human trafficking, and become fugitives from the law and from the corporations.

Iulia Sexta, the younger of the two sisters, is suffering from an identity crisis. Is it gender dysphoria? Was she supposed to be a man? Is that why she likes girls? Or is a ghost from one of her previous lives now trying to haunt his way back into the living by taking over her body and mind?

With both the past and the present pursuing them, Iulia Tertia and Iulia Sexta find their future under constant attack. Doing the right thing is not only difficult at best, but may well result in their deaths. What to do? One thing at a time...

Order and read the adventure of a lifetime!

https://www.hiraethsffh.com/product-page/iuliae-past-tense-by-tyree-campbell

The Sisterhood of the Blood Moon
By Terrie Leigh Relf

For thousands of Earth years, the Transgalactic Consortium has had an invested interest in this planet and its inhabitants, the Haurans. While the Sisterhood of the Blood Moon and the Guardians work together with the Consortium and Haurans to restore balance to the universe, the Blood Moon is fast approaching. The power of this moon reveals untold secrets . . . including the sacred covenant with the Mora Spiders. There is an ancient pact that continues to be honored – but at what cost and for whose purpose?

The world may come to an end. But will there be a chance for a new beginning? And if so, where?

Find out! Order a copy now!

https://www.hiraethsffh.com/product-page/sisterhood-of-the-blood-moon-by-terrie-leigh-relf

Space Port Duty-Free Drabbler

from the desk of the Boortean Ambassador . . .

Greetings, Spacefarers and Dear Friends of Boort!

While you're traveling between or within star systems, working aboard space stations and ports, or otherwise engaged in various activities, there's an excellent chance that you will stop by the duty-free malls and shops. Whether you're looking for the perfect gift for your podlings, hoping to grab a memento to remember your adventures (or dare I say it . . . attempting to smuggle various types of contraband in or out), space stations are an intriguing place.

Thank you to all the travelers who have shared their experience (and long-live the Resistance!).

Until next time,
Your humble ambassador,
Terrie Leigh Relf

Somehow We've Got to Force the Legislature to Clamp Down on These Human Trafficking Companies
Francis W. Alexander

Something still isn't right. Either women are spawning babies like crazy and some substance is growing them fast, or someone has devised a new method of smuggling workers.

Last week, Barney Knewman discovered that zombified slaves were using fake id cards. He got fired for taking so long to catch them.

Here is another one wearing a tight red hat. He looks at me with small beady eyes.

I scan him with the Truthilizer3 beam.

His cap rises and leaps off his head. Wires stick out of the skull.

"Get that shapeshifter!" I shout as it dashes out the door.

A Hair-Brained Scheme
Christine Whitten

"Welcome to Earth. Passport?" asked the Immigration Agent, yawning with eyes closed. His eyes opened, then panned upward scrutinizing the 8-foot green Denebian's four arms, two tentacles, and head of furry hair.

Startled, the Agent frowned. "Aren't all Denebs hairless?"

The giant scowled, arms and tentacles crossed. "Are you mocking my deformity?"

The agent shrank. "Uh, no SIR!" he sputtered. He glanced at the declaration. "No off-world animals to declare, I see," stamping it quickly. "Enjoy your stay."

Leaving Spaceport, the Denebian unwrapped the fluffy, two-headed creature from his bald head, caressing it with his tentacles. "Good girl," he cooed.

Honorable Mention

Spacestation Romeo
Tom Duke

Well, I've haunted Spaceport Echo-Niner for eight weeks now—smuggled my ectoplasmic self aboard during the last crew changeover. I lost my final cat-life back on SPE-4 (an unfortunate airlock mishap), and I've been port hopping ever since. But here's the coolest part, I discovered Echo-Niner is already haunted by a cute gray tabby ghost named Kaz, with the fluffiest tail I've ever seen! She was a bit standoffish at first, but my sublime wit and charm quickly won her over. Now we're so close we share shadows (ghost humor).

—From the journal of Spytz, the Gypsy Cat Space Ghost—

Blood Price:
A young adult superhero novella

Blood Price prowls the alleys . . .

"The cat hissed, its attention focused on something approaching her from behind. Blood Price spun around fast enough to take the hit from the front, but her attacker still knocked her flat. It reminded her of pictures she'd seen of black jaguars, but its body was smaller, its snout was blunter, and there were patches in its coat through which she could see muscle and bone.

At the moment, however, both her mind and her hands were occupied as she grasped it by the neck, **keeping its teeth away from her throat . . ."**

By day she's Penny Price, sixteen, related to an industrialist, wanting to do something important with her life. By night she's Blood Price, attired in purple tights and a domino mask, fighting chaos and the beasties that emerge to cause chaos. With the help of a wolfboy and a magic girl and a ghost, she takes on all adversaries. But one day . . . well, but that would spoil it.

Ordering Link:
Print Edition:
https://www.hiraethsffh.com/product-page/blood-price-by-martin-white

Entry Denied
Joseph Sidari

The Antarean customs agent waggled a pseudopod at me. "Smuggling hazardous material from Earth is illegal."

My stomach plunged. I'd spent years arranging today's meeting with their ruling caste to present democratic principles to improve the lives of all Antareans. Currently, they have no elections. No free speech. Not even trial by jury.

"But you scanned my luggage when my starship docked. I've no weapons, toxins, microbes, or genetic contaminants." The laws on Antares were inviolable. It'd be suicide to transport contraband.

"We scanned your mind," said the agent. "You have dangerous ideas. It's the subterranean work camps for you."

The Perfect Duty-Free Gift
Margarida Brei

Jellied suncat gave me indigestion. Rainbow alcohol fizzled my brains. Hippy slimeballs caused constipation. Abruptly, I saw the perfect gift in the space station duty-free. Grow your own human. Excited, I read the label-lifelike, original size, realistic. Blonde, ginger or brunette. I left the kit to be animated by storms. The lightning nurtured its shapely sexiness. Later, I gasped! Beautiful! Feminine! A perfect wife for a lonesome alien. Then she opened her mouth to a tsunami of abuse and nagging.

The duty-free agent dismissed my no-return receipt with, "Enjoy."

Females must be the reason aliens do not invade earth.

To the Shore, to the Sea
By Erica Ruppert

An alien invasion changes human life on Earth. Their ships disintegrate on Earth, leaking poisons into the soil. The aliens take to the seas. With nowhere for people to go, many perish. Tansy and Luke take their daughter Maria to their family home by the ocean, seeking refuge. But there are strange creatures in the water, and they have a siren's call that is irresistible and unavoidable.

Things change at the shore. Inexplicably, children are hungry all the time. And already it is too late…

To lose a loved one to Death is almost unbearable. But to lose a loved one still living, and changing because of the aliens, requires a surrender no one is prepared to make.

Ordering links:
Print: https://www.hiraethsffh.com/product-page/to-the-shore-to-the-sea-by-erica-ruppert

ePub: https://www.hiraethsffh.com/product-page/to-the-shore-to-the-sea-by-erica-ruppert-2

PDF: https://www.hiraethsffh.com/product-page/to-the-shore-to-the-sea-by-erica-ruppert-1

And now a word from a new sponsor . . .

(Brought to YOU by the Boortean Ambassador)

Suki's Surveillance Systems™

Space stations can be exciting, and let's face it, dangerous places. In addition to trans-galactic tourists, temporary-and-long-term residents, as well as assorted staff (then there's the soaring turnover rate), you may have spies, smugglers, thieves, and yes, revolutionaries and counterrevolutionaries. Can your security teams investigate every lead or incident? Can your incarceration facilities house everyone that commits an infraction? This is why installing a station-wide internal-and- external surveillance system is the answer.

Disclaimer: This is NOT your usual surveillance system. Due to the proprietary nature of our system, you will need to sign a non-disclosure agreement prior to discussing terms.

Alpha Centauri Space Station Duty-Free: Incident Register
Charlotte Kowalski

0600 Store open.

0612 Minor tussle between Ardorian and Palanian over last stuffed toy kangaroo. Minor tentacle bruising.

0745 Ardorian youth caught shoplifting. Three building block sets retrieved from abdominal pouch.

1022 Medical staff called to attend to Cyanese female with severe allergic reaction to perfume sample.

1305 Security escorted Palanian male to exit after outburst regarding the import ban of chocolate macadamias to Palania.

1657 Cleaners called to mop up faintly glowing blue goop in candy aisle.

1939 Music system caused overload on Cyanese tablet device. Song playing at the time was "Macarena." Insurance claim filed.

2003 Store closed.

Coyote
Jeff Currier

Jatri's transmat logs, scrolling across Talib's iGlasses, showed nothing—no hidden tech, sub-dermal compartments, anomalous substances . . . so what was Jatri smuggling? Outside Customs Interview 3, Talib tried guessing today's tic—giggling? Impassiveness? Teeth grinding? Talib swiped the door.

"Talib! Long time no see; how's it hanging?"

Gregariousness, Talib decided. He displayed Jatri's vial pack.

"What's this?"

"Usual—EZClone genetic samples.

"Whose?"

"I'm just the courier agent-man. Ain't no mule—transmat log's clean, right."

* * *

Jatri's clearance imminent, Talib pondered—known smuggler, changing mannerisms, clones. What if . . .

He opened Jatri's last five transmat logs. Brain patterns all different. Gotcha! Bastard's smuggling consciousnesses.

A Million Holes: Einstein Would Be Proud
Gary Davis

Exiled galactic warlord Zondyr entered NASA Space Station *Einstein* in disguise, orbiting above Titan. His army of a million mini-android soldiers hovered invisibly outside. Each soldier was made of antimatter and downsized to a comic dust speck. Zondyr had discovered the antimatter within nebulas near the center of the Milky Way. His antimatter space force soon rushed to isolated outer walls of *Einstein Station* and quietly tunneled micro-millimeter holes to the inside, then patched them up with matter dust particles floating within the station.

Zondyr's army, entering duty-free, was ready to attack. Humans would now be the ones to pay.

Living Bad Dreams
By Denise Hatfield

When dreams come alive, there's no telling where they will lead. Everything changes when you realize that, dream or no dream, you're going to die. What do you do then?

Ordering Link:
Print Edition:
https://www.hiraethsffh.com/product-page/living-bad-dreams-by-denise-hatfield-1
ePub Edition:
https://www.hiraethsffh.com/product-page/living-bad-dreams-by-denise-hatfield-2
PDF Edition:
https://www.hiraethsffh.com/product-page/living-bad-dreams-by-denise-hatfield

Synapsers
Denise Hatfield

Brains are a delicacy on some planets. So, when the opportunity presented itself to commandeer a shipment headed for the Planet of The Dead, well, I couldn't resist. As an Octiper, I designed my craft and it is comparable to none. With its Inkjet Cloaking Device and 707 Warp Drive, you'll never see or catch me. Becoming a smuggler just made sense and the money well worth it. I'm headed to Earth with the Synapsers. I saved them from extinction; they need new hosts, and Earth needs brains that function. Today, everybody wins. Even a smuggler can do charity occasionally.

The Rough Side of Space
Marcia A. Borell

Our space station is held together by paperclips, chewing gum, and prayers. In ancient times it would have been called MacGyvered! So was my store. Crates became display tables, old computer parts became jewelry, and trades were welcome.

The last trade I made was iffy. It was a steel rod with pretty designs carved into it. It had needed a good polish, so I took it to my quarters. I left Edna in charge.

Edna is now nothing but a patch of scorched flooring, and I have a threatening note: Give me back my wand, or else!

Finders Keepers!

Mine!

Gizm-oh-no-you-DON'T!
Kristin Lennox Mill

I am Father of the Freakin' Year...

Lewis smiled smugly as the customs line snaked through *Joro Colony* spaceport. He had his son's birthday in the bag. Or in his stomach, actually.

"Please bring back a Gizmodo, Daddy—everyone has one!"

Now, thanks to an AtomScaler, the spiny reptile was resting in comfortable stasis in a small capsule in Lewis' stomach. No customs tax, no quarantine, no Alien Pet registry...

"Step in, please, sir." *Just the Biometric Validation machine, stay cool...*

As the machine's resizer component kicked in, the butterflies in Lewis' stomach were obliterated by a full-sized, hungry Gizmodo.

Honorable Mention

Caveat Emptor
Greg Schwartz

Chitilictl darted through the spaceport, crashing into travelers (and walls). He needed somewhere to stash the Altarian Key. Half the galaxy was hunting for it, but his immediate concern was the Xalabashian mercenary chasing him.

He ducked into a gift shop. He slit open a pink plush rock monster, stuffed the key inside, and tossed it into a corner. He skittered out, disappearing into the crowd. He'd return after losing the soldier.

* * *

Walking to his terminal, Bulplatazar passed a duty-free shop. He poked his head in, wanting a present for his daughter. He grabbed the first pink thing he saw.

Introducing one of our newest sponsors (Brought to YOU by The Boortean Ambassador)

K'tek's Multiphasic Monitoring Services™

Are you concerned by the number of clandestine operations occurring on your space station? Have you discovered that your personnel and electronic devices aren't sufficient to catch individuals with unapproved (and dangerous) thoughts, feelings, and ideations? What about consciousness and contraband smugglers? Look no further than K'tek's Multiphasic Monitoring Services™. Our team of telepaths, empaths, Mind Grid Walkers, and former members of The Sisterhood of the Blood Moon are here to ensure that the resistance will survive! Just imagine restoring equilibrium to your planet and its surrounding moons! Just imagine restoring peace and prosperity within your trans-galactic enterprises. Just imagine . . .

Contraband
Scott O'Neill

"Anything to declare?"

The Sol-3 Global Socialist Republic customs officer just stares. I feel like a bug pinned to a card. They take entire courses learning that stare, same as the secret police.

I shake my head.

I'm scanned. 3D mapped. Spectrally analyzed. A brutally efficient neural-net AI catalogues my thoughts.

Finally, I'm pronounced fit to mingle with Earth's proletariat. I'm waved through.

They missed it.

Buried in the memory of nearly drowning as a child, my illicit cargo lurks. A weapons-grade cache of hope and optimism.

Stifling a smile, I hurry to the shuttle, and my waiting Resistance contacts.

Nothing to Declare
Greg Beatty

When the airlock cycled open, De'Von called, "Welcome to LaGrange 3. Anything to declare?"

There was no answer.

After a while, De'Von muttered to his coworker, "I thought maintenance fixed that door."

There was no answer. Ze'Tar was lying in a heap on the deck.

Using reflexes honed through training and years in space, De'Von slapped the emergency button and moved toward his fellow customs agent.

Then, with a cough and a wince, De'Von joined Ze'Tar in unconsciousness.

The airlock door cycled closed, and soon, no one had anything to declare in the entire space station. No one at all.

Duty-Free Import?
D. L. R. Frase

Looking up, Earth Station Customs Agent Matheson asked, "Anything to declare?"

Unxor scowled. "Declare? This is an outrage!"

Nodding, the agent hoisted Unxor's suitcase onto the table. "Yeah, we'll see about that."

Clenching his jaws, Unxor growled, "I'm a tourist here for a day visit."

His statement was ignored as Matheson flipped the lid open.

The case held only a cage containing a furry four-legged animal.

In seconds, Station Security surrounded Unxor.

Matheson snatched up Unxor's papers and continued, "Smuggling an exotic animal to Earth duty-free is a serious crime."

Enraged, Unxor screamed, "That's no exotic animal! That's my lunch!"

SECOND PLACE

Two Customs Agents Settle a Regulatory Dispute
Roger Johns

"The embargo applies only to memories. Those aren't memories."

"Even though they're stored in her hippocampus?"

"They're not covered by the regulation, unless they can be summoned into conscious awareness. She won't be able to recall those because they're locked inside encrypted psychiatric shielding."

"But the subject matter scan indicates strong congruence with highly malignant, messianic thought patterns."

"Psych shielding renders conceptual content irrelevant."

"You can't let her onto the planet. Rogue neuros could uncloak that information."

"They'd have to know it's there."

"Shouldn't we assume—"

"—they've been expecting her? Of course." I raise my blaster. "Sometimes, change is good."

https://www.hiraethsffh.com/product-page/woman-from-the-institute-by-tyree-campbell

FIRST PLACE

If I Could Save Time in A Bottle
Iseult Murphy

Celeste bought a souvenir from every space station she visited. She knew it was kind of hokey, but she loved the little temporal spheres that preserved worlds in time locked bubbles.

It surprised her to see her homeworld of Artemis shining like a vermillion pearl on the seller's display beams.

"How did this get here?"

"All clearance planets, stored to make way for new sub-space corridor. Better than being destroyed."

It was expensive, but worth it.

She hadn't seen her family in years, but she hoped if they looked at the sky, they might glimpse her looking down at them.

Down to Earth
N.E. Rule

On re-entry to the space station, the guard examines my customs form. Can he hear my heart pounding?

"Nothing to declare?" His voice bored.

"Nope," I hold tight to the piece of history in my pocket.

"No red dust from Mars?"

"No! People still smoke that shit?" I laugh.

"Or, love rocks from Venus?" He's watching me.

I'd pay the duty if it could pass for that. But not taking a chance, I shake my head.

His eyes narrow. "Taking souvenirs from Earth while it's regenerating is illegal."

Sighing, I hand over a blue, petrified chunk of the Pacific Ocean.

Welcome to T'lar's Duty-Free Mall on the *Anemone* Space Station
By T'lar

That right. T'lar take back duty-free mall from lazy cousins. They no make profit from space tourists or other travelers. If T'lar find out they steal, out airlock. T'lar have great deals for customers. More you buy, more you save. Duty-free. Come to *Anemone* station and get good deals on Mora silk and honey. Podlings love Mora honey. T'lar have Hauran toys on sale now. That said, T'lar know some items not legal in other quadrants, so T'lar have associates create unique packaging. Have special price for dignitaries like Boortean Ambassador. She appreciate Tyraelian brandy and grant favors to T'lar.

The Trafficking of TEs by Reen Trusteven's Subordinate
sakyu

Ex-convict Peageen Tennor eyed the holding-cell of telempathic draftees, searching. Charged with selecting one of them for his employer's growing cache of illegal slaves, he was looking for a young TE that wouldn't put up much of a fight.

He'd successfully performed this duty several times. The valuable draftees were kept locked up for their own protection, but there was always a way around those things, and Peageen was adept at finding them.

His gaze locked on a young girl-child, and his features slid into a slow grin. Perfect.

In moments they were away. He'd be handsomely rewarded for this.

Adopted Child
By Teri Santitoro
(aka sakyu)

Imp, now 13, has awakened from stasis by MA, the ship's computer, to find that everyone else has been killed by a highly infectious disease. She is alone on the ship. But she is about to have visitors.

The *Greentown*, a salvage ship, has spotted a derelict and is about to board her for salvage rights. The crew is blissfully unaware of what happened to the people on the derelict. Soon enough they will find out...but will it be too late? And what of the girl who now controls the derelict?

To everyone involved, everything is new...and potentially lethal.

Ordering Links:
Print Edition ($9.00):
https://www.hiraethsffh.com/product-page/adopted-child-by-t-santitoro

PDF Edition ($3.99):
https://www.hiraethsffh.com/product-page/adopted-child-by-t-santitoro-1

And NOW a final word from our most-esteemed sponsor (Brought to YOU by The Boortean Ambassador)

Coming to a Space Port Near You Soon: T'lar's Terrarium and Exotic Plant Store

T'lar's life partner, Nami, have great idea. We open chain of terrarium and exotic plant stores throughout quadrant. Then you have something beautiful to remember travels. Nami says they good gifts. We have all sizes: Small, medium, large, extra-large. Just imagine Mora blossoms* on tea table in living space. Just imagine miniature Tyraelian nut trees on food preparation counter. Just imagine entire wall of Mahrainian Tuka fruit. You get idea. We make terrariums or you make yourself.

Disclaimer: T'lar and Nami not responsible if Mora spiders get loose in living quarters. Contact Sisterhood of Blood Moon if spider bite you.

END OF TRANSMISSION

www.ingramcontent.com/pod-product-compliance
Lightning Source LLC
LaVergne TN
LVHW051926060526
838201LV00062B/4706